The Stupid Ogre

An Italian folk tale

retold by Rosalind Kerven
Illustrated by Georgie Birkett

OXFORD
UNIVERSITY PRESS

Once upon a time, a boy called
Mario bought a big bag of oranges.

He climbed up a tree.
He started to eat one of his oranges.

Just then, a big bad ogre came along.

The ogre looked up at Mario.

The ogre loved food.
He liked oranges, but his favourite
food was boys!

"I want an orange!" shouted the ogre.
"Come down and give me one."

Mario climbed down.
He put an orange into the ogre's
hand.

The ogre grabbed the orange,
and then he grabbed Mario!

"Help! Help!" shouted Mario.
The ogre pushed Mario into his sack.

He picked up the sack and went
home.

The ogre stopped for a drink.
He put the sack down.

Mario peeped out and saw that
the ogre wasn't looking.
He jumped out of the sack.

Mario filled the sack with stones.
Then he ran away.

The ogre picked up the sack and took it home to his wife.

"Wife! Wife!" shouted the ogre.
"I've got a nice boy for us to eat!"
His wife looked in the sack.

"You stupid old ogre," she said.
"There is no boy in here.
   This sack is full of stones."

The ogre was very cross.
"I'm going to get that boy!" he said.

The ogre could not climb the tree.
"How did you get up that tree?"
he shouted to Mario.

"I made a pile of pots and pans and
cups and glasses," said Mario.
"Then I climbed up it."

"You could make a big pile too,"
said Mario.
The ogre ran home.

The ogre got lots of pots and pans and cups and glasses.

He made a big pile.
He started to climb up the pile.

The ogre never tried to eat Mario again.